Secrets of a
Small Brother

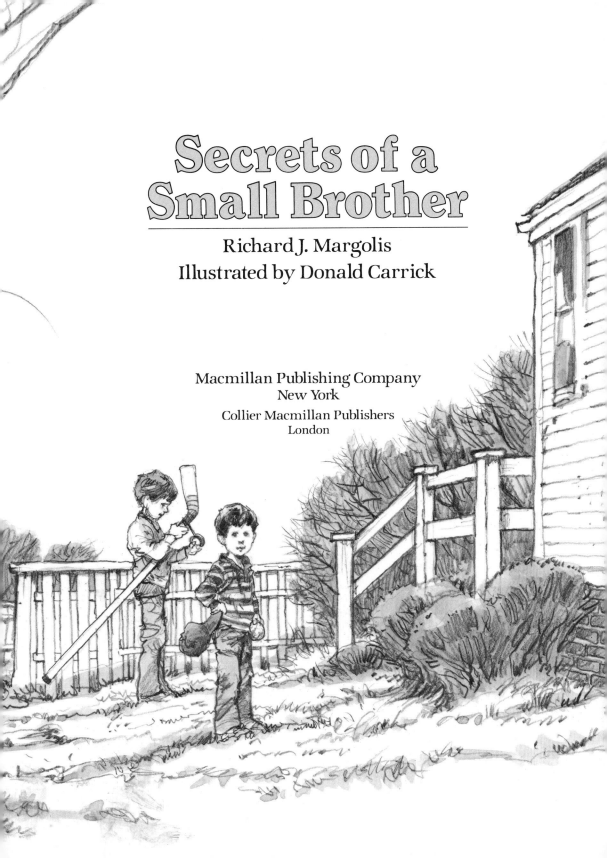

Secrets of a Small Brother

Richard J. Margolis
Illustrated by Donald Carrick

Macmillan Publishing Company
New York
Collier Macmillan Publishers
London

Copyright © 1984 Richard J. Margolis
Copyright © 1984 Donald Carrick
All rights reserved. No part of this book may be reproduced
or transmitted in any form or by any means, electronic or
mechanical, including photocopying, recording or by any
information storage and retrieval system, without
permission in writing from the Publisher.

Macmillan Publishing Company
866 Third Avenue, New York, N.Y. 10022
Collier Macmillan Canada, Inc.
Printed in the United States of America
10 9 8 7 6 5 4 3
Library of Congress Cataloging in Publication Data
Margolis, Richard J.
Secrets of a small brother.
Summary: A series of poems reveal a young boy's
relationship with his older brother.
1. Brothers—Juvenile poetry. 2. Children's poetry,
American. [1. Brothers—Poetry. 2. American poetry]
I. Carrick, Donald, ill. II. Title.
PS3563.A65S4   1984   811'.54   84-3878
ISBN 0-02-762280-0

For Phil, my big brother
—*R. J. M.*

To Eddie and Michael
—*D. C.*

SCHOOL MORNINGS

On school days he gets up first.
The lamp glares.
The floor groans.
The faucet spits.
The hangers in our closet clang.
When my bed shakes,
I know he is tying his shoe.
Time to get up.

LESSONS

My teacher taught me to add
and I tried it on Dad.
He taught me to subtract
and I tried it on Gram.
She taught me to spell
and I tried it on my brother.
He taught me a new word
and I tried it on Mom.
She washed my mouth out with salt water.

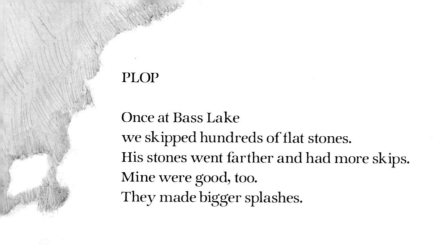

PLOP

Once at Bass Lake
we skipped hundreds of flat stones.
His stones went farther and had more skips.
Mine were good, too.
They made bigger splashes.

ALL MY HATS

All my hats
are hats he wore.
What a bore.

All my pants
are pants he ripped.
What a gyp.

All my books
are books he read.
What a head.

All my fights
are fights he fought.
What a thought.

All my steps
are steps he tried.
What a guide.

All my teachers
call me by my brother's name.
What a shame.

DINNERTIME

Slowly slowly
glides his hand beneath the table.
I see his fingers
clutch a corner of my napkin.
Gently gently
slides the napkin off my lap.
I pounce.
Gotcha!

    You two better stop that.
    Stop what?
    Stop whatever it is you're doing.
    We're not doing anything.
    Then stop whatever it is you're not doing.
    Geez.

Slowly slowly
glides my hand beneath the table.
My fingers grope.
Gently gently
slides the napkin ....

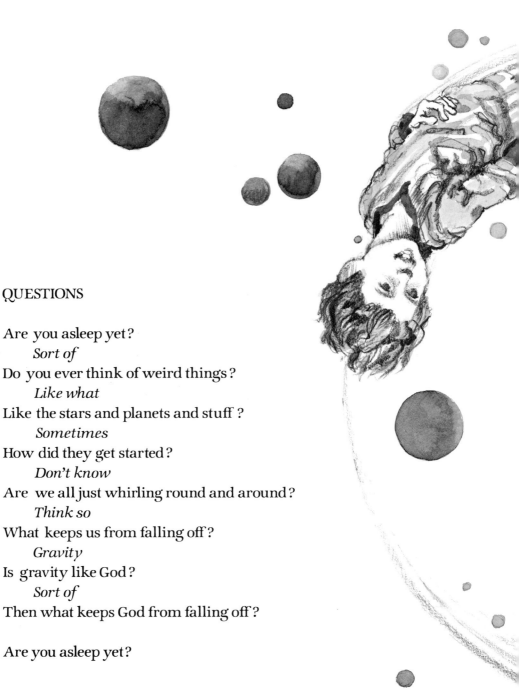

QUESTIONS

Are you asleep yet?
    Sort of
Do you ever think of weird things?
    Like what
Like the stars and planets and stuff?
    Sometimes
How did they get started?
    Don't know
Are we all just whirling round and around?
    Think so
What keeps us from falling off?
    Gravity
Is gravity like God?
    Sort of
Then what keeps God from falling off?

Are you asleep yet?

COLD POTATO

To be a second class scout
you have to pass cooking.
My brother and me,
we make a fire in the backyard
and I shove a potato inside.
When it gets all black
I roll it out with a stick.
"It's hard like a baseball," I say.
"You cooked it, you eat it," he says.

There's a lot you have to swallow
when your brother's the patrol leader.

HIS DOG

My brother shuffles through the door
carrying little Sandy in his arms.
His tears make Sandy's fur wet.
When I try to pet her head,
he pulls away. "Don't," he says.
"She's dead."
Then I pet my brother's head.
She was his dog.

TEASED

Sometimes
when I'm teased
I don't cry,
I go away.
When I come back
my brother and his friends
are doing something else.
I remember.
They forget.

DOWNHILL

This time let *me* steer
and you be in back.
Do my feet go here?
Do I follow this track?
No no, I'm really okay,
I know what I'm doing.
Hang on tight.... Hey!
We're going, we're going.
Everything's white.
Everything's slick.
Lean to the right—
I mean the left. Quick.
Look out, look out. Jump!

This is the lousiest sled I've ever seen.
Next time you be in front
and I'll lean.

SOUPS AND JUICES

Did you hear about my big brother?
The lucky stiff is sick.
All day they bring him soups and juices.
When he calls, they come running.
They keep puffing his pillow.

I'm supposed to stay out
but tonight I peeked in.
He was asleep.
The dumb kid
kicked off his blankets
so I went and covered him up.
He looked *small*.

UNCLE JULIUS

My Uncle Julius died.
His hands were bony
and his chin was rough.
He gave me a dollar once.
When our telephone split the dark
I could see the sound:
saw-toothed lightning.
Then I opened my eyes
and heard Gram crying.
"Juliekin, my Juliekin."
Long ago they lived together.
He was her little brother.

LAST WORD

I have this neat truck
I race along the floor.
One time it trips my brother.
"Toy trucks are for babies," he says,
hiding it from me. Do I scream!
That night, trying to sleep,
I see my brother kneeling on his bed.
He is pushing my truck
along the blanket and over the pillow.
" You're a baby, " I whisper, and fall asleep.

BIRTHDAY

Today I'm a year older
and he isn't.
I'm getting closer all the time.
If he skipped just two birthdays
while I was catching up,
we'd be even.
It wouldn't be so tough on him.
I'd give him presents anyway.

WHERE AM I?

"Go back to where we left the bikes
and get the sandwiches.
Do you remember the way?"
"Yah."
"You sure?"
"I said yah, didn't I?"

I enter the dark woods.
The bikes must be this way,
or maybe *this* way.
All the rocks and trees look alike.
Forget the bikes ... find my brother.
I slip in mud
and stumble through pricklies.
Then I see him in our clearing.
He is standing on a big rock,
turning in all directions.
He is eating a sandwich.

My brother glares at me.
"Where you been? You were gone
so long I went back to find you."
I take off my wet socks and shoes
and glare at my brother.
"Gimme a peanut butter."

NIGHT EYES

From my brother's bed
we watch the night train
glimmer down the long valley.
The passengers,
they're in bed, too,
wondering if we're watching.
We are all moving.
We are all night eyes.

CAN'T WIN

"Which one of you did this?"
my mother asks, picking up the pieces.
I start to say me
but my brother's stare
shuts my mouth.
"Well, if neither of you can speak,
both of you can go without candy this week."

I wish my brother wouldn't do me favors.
No candy, and still I owe him one.

TWO WHEELS

I told you I won't. It's too hard.
I told you I can't. It's too hard.
Didn't I tell you?

My feet, they won't reach.
My hands, they won't steer.
It's too hard.

Watch out—I'm tipping.
Don't let go—I'm falling.
Please: I give up.

Not so fast, not so fast.
I don't like this.
Stop stop stop stop.

Hey, I can't stop.
Hey, I'm riding, I'm riding.
Hey hey hey hey hey.

Did you see me?
What did I tell you?
It was easy.

ON THE SIDELINES

Sometimes when I watch my brother
come to bat,
my feelings don't know what I want.
He hits one a mile
and I feel grumpy as I cheer.
He strikes out
and I feel cheerful as I groan.
What do my feelings want from me?
To *bat*,
that's what.

REGRETS

The time my brother
got his jacket hooked
along the crossbar
in the playground,
flopping like a puppet,
yipping like a puppy,
all his friends
just stood around and laughed.
I should have kicked them.

A JULY GOODBYE

Take your duffel bag and go.
I'm tired of tripping on
that stuffed July of yours:
the pocket knife, the bent canteen,
those scratchy woolen blankets for your bunk.
What junk.

You'll be in the movie now,
the one Mr. Finster flashes every fall
against our kitchen wall.
We'll watch you squinting in the sun,
hiking the woods, shooting the rapids,
while old Finster's film hums and hums.
Flicker flicker wave wave.

Who will your bunk mate be?
Don't tell me.
I have other things to think about
these fourteen unstuffed days.
(Fifteen, if you count the day we bring you back.)

ONE PURPLE SUMMER EVE

One purple summer eve
our dinghy tips
and I fall through the glassy lake.
Down down down down
sleepily down a jellied slope.
Hold your breath. Hold your brain.
Hold everything.
Up up up up
dreamily up a murmuring tunnel.
The sky bursts. The air shouts.
In the glare I kick hard,
stretching toward my brother's hand.